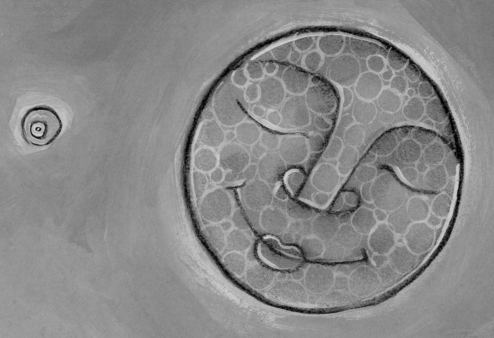

De Colores

BRIGHT WITH COLORS

pictures by

David Diaz

Marshall Cavendish Children

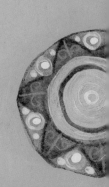

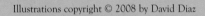

Marshall Cavendish Corporation
99 White Plains Road
Tarrytown, NY 10591
www.marshallcavendish.us/kids

Library of Congress Cataloging-in-Publication Data
De colores — Bright with colors / illustrated by David Diaz. — 1st ed.
    p. cm.
  Spanish and English words.
  Includes music score.
  ISBN 978-0-7614-5431-1 (alk. paper)
  1. Children's songs, Spanish. 2. Children's songs, English.
  I. Diaz, David. ill II. Title: Bright with colors.
M1998 .D
782.42'0268—dc22

                              2007022133

The text of this book is set in Goudy Old Style.
The illustrations were rendered in acrylic, pencil, and colored pencil.
Book design by Vera Soki
Editor: Margery Cuyler

Printed in China
First edition
1 3 5 6 4 2

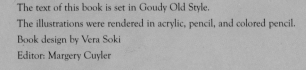

for
Buttercup
D.D.

De colores,
de colores se visten los campos
en la primavera.

De colores,
bright with colors the mountains
and valleys dress up
in the springtime.

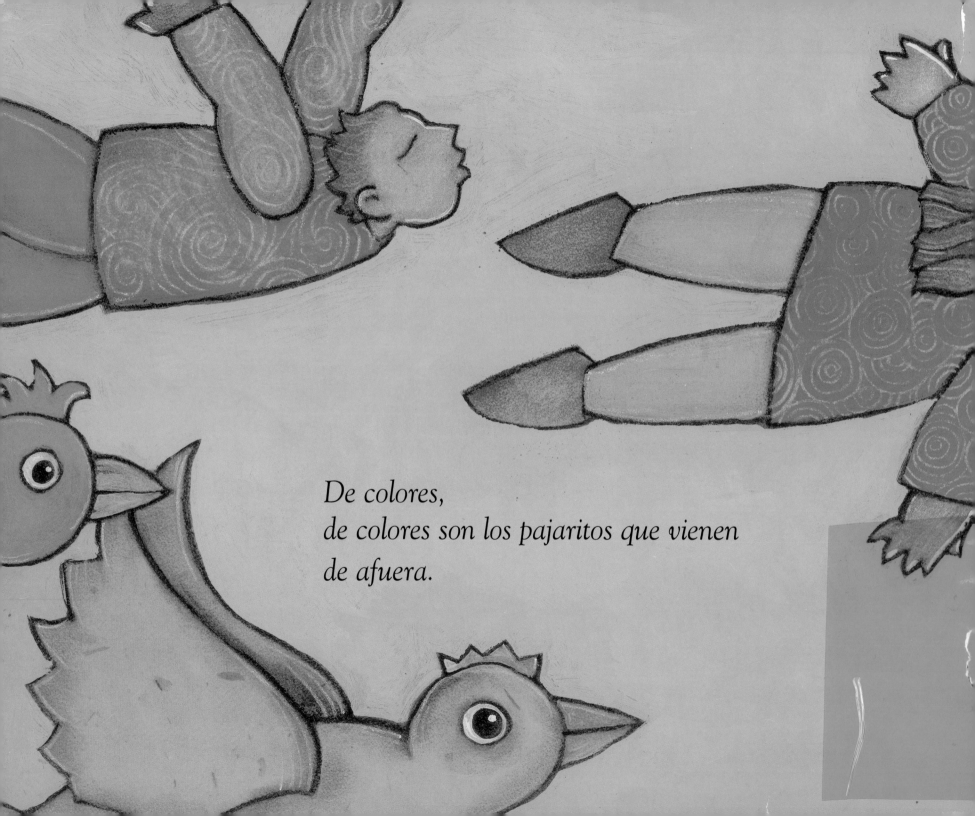

De colores,
de colores son los pajaritos que vienen
de afuera.

De colores,
bright with colors all the little birds
fill the skies in the daytime.

De colores,
de colores es el arco iris que
vemos lucir.

De colores,
bright with colors the rainbow brings joy
with the glory of spring.

Y por eso los grandes amores
de muchos colores me gustan
a mí.

And a bright love has found us
with peace all around us
that makes our hearts sing.

Y por eso los grandes amores
de muchos colores me gustan
a mí.

And a bright love has found us
with peace all around us
that makes our hearts sing.

Canta el gallo,
canta el gallo con el quirí, quirí, quirí, quirí, quirí.

Sings the rooster,
sings the rooster with his *kiri, kiri, kiri, kiri, kiri.*

La gallina,
la gallina con el cara, cara, cara, cara, cara.

And the cluck hen,
and the cluck hen with her *cara, cara, cara, cara, cara.*

Los polluelos,
los polluelos con el pío, pío, pío, pío, pí.

And the baby chicks,
and the baby chicks with their *pío, pío, pío, pío, pí*.

Y por eso los grandes amores
de muchos colores me gustan
a mí.

And a bright love has found us
with peace all around us
that makes our hearts sing.

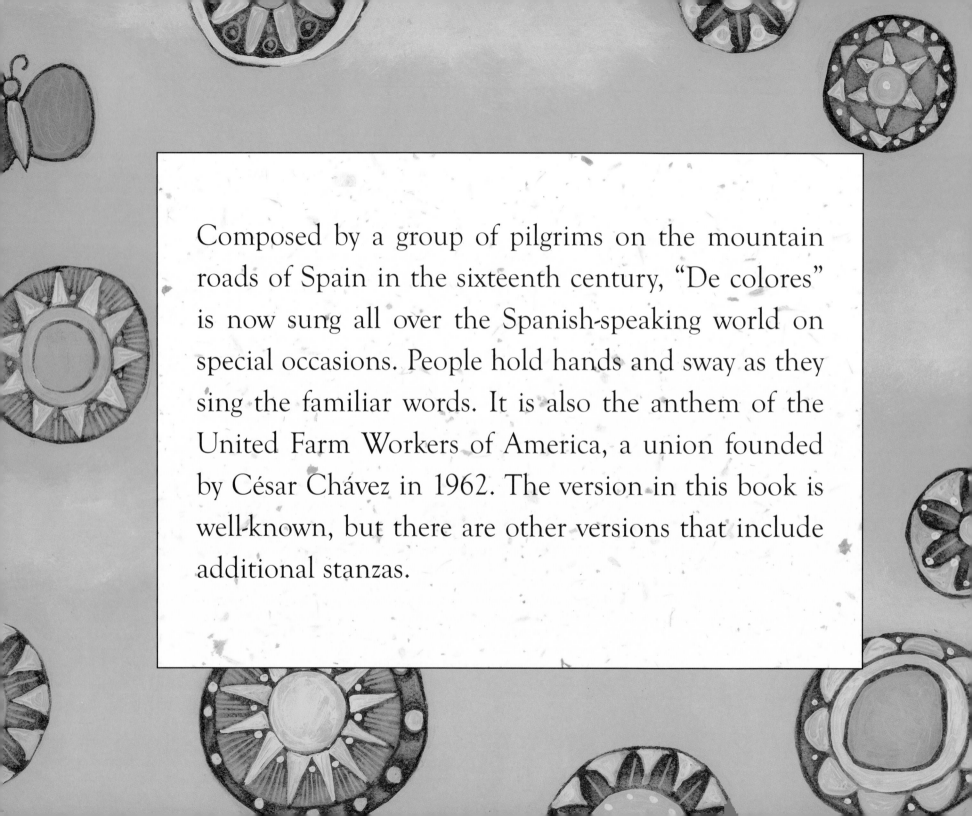

Composed by a group of pilgrims on the mountain roads of Spain in the sixteenth century, "De colores" is now sung all over the Spanish-speaking world on special occasions. People hold hands and sway as they sing the familiar words. It is also the anthem of the United Farm Workers of America, a union founded by César Chávez in 1962. The version in this book is well-known, but there are other versions that include additional stanzas.